CINCO DE MOUSE-O!

by **Judy Cox**

illustrated by
Jeffrey Ebbeler

Holiday House / New York

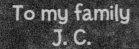

To my family
J. C.

For Fritz
J. E.

Cinco de Mayo
(the fifth of May) is an
important day in Mexican
and Latino communities.
The holiday commemorates
the victory of the
Mexican army over the
French in the Battle of
Puebla, in Mexico, in 1862
and is an opportunity to
celebrate Mexican and
Latino cultural
traditions.

The publisher
would like to thank
Lena Burgos-Lafuente
of New York University's
Department of Spanish
and Portuguese for reviewing
the Spanish in this book for accuracy.

HOLIDAY HOUSE is registered in the U.S. Patent and Trademark Office.
Printed and Bound in October 2009 in Johor Bahru, Johor, Malaysia, at Tien Wah Press.
The text typeface is Billy Regular.
The artwork was created with acrylic paint, pastels, and colored pencil on paper.
www.holidayhouse.com
First Edition
1 3 5 7 9 10 8 6 4 2

Library of Congress Cataloging-in-Publication Data
Cox, Judy.
Cinco de Mouse-O! / by Judy Cox ; illustrated by Jeffrey Ebbeler. — 1st ed.
p. cm.
Summary: Mouse enjoys the sights and smells of Cinco de Mayo
despite being trailed by a determined cat.
ISBN 978-0-8234-2194-7 (hardcover)
[1. Mice—Fiction. 2. Cinco de Mayo (Mexican holiday)—Fiction.]
I. Ebbeler, Jeffrey, ill. II. Title.
PZ7.C83835Cin 2010
[E]—dc22
2008048463

On the fifth of May, Mouse woke up and wriggled his whiskers. Spicy smells tickled his nose—beany, cheesy, ricey smells. A Mexican fiesta. *¡Fantástico!*

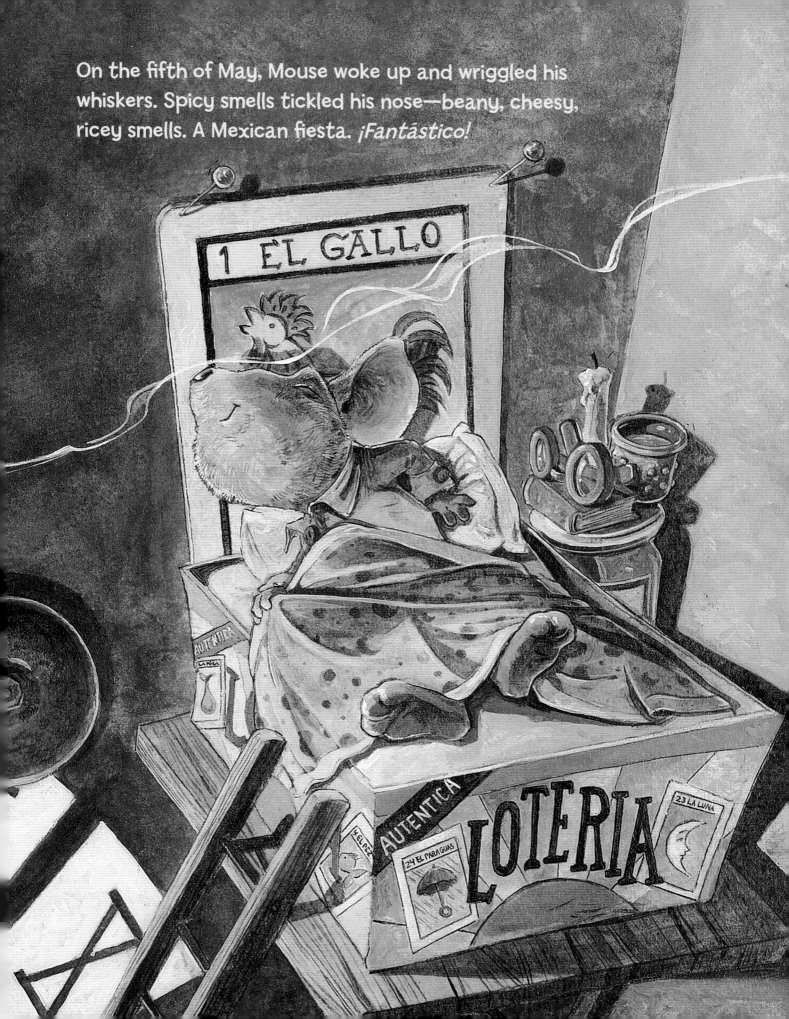

Mouse crawled out of
his hidey-hole. Where was
the fiesta? Not in the
bathroom where the kids
brushed their teeth.
Not in the bedroom
where Mom folded
laundry.

Not in the kitchen where Dad washed dishes. Mouse slipped out the front door and set off to explore.

Mouse scampered down alleyways, past sidewalks and streetlights. He didn't see greedy Cat stalk him down the street.
Before long, Mouse stopped at the edge of the city park.

What sights met his eyes! All around were people eating, singing, dancing, strolling, playing. All around were food and drink, sombreros, serapes, and bright paper flowers. **¡Cinco de Mayo!**

His eyes grew round as he beheld a confetti-covered piñata, stuffed with candy and shaped like a burro, hanging in a tree above the plaza.

"I must have that for my fiesta," he said to himself. He jumped, but the enticing piñata swung far out of reach.

But all around were people eating, dropping snacks for mouse-sized meals! Yummy foods he'd never tasted before! Tacos, tamales, chorizos, and flan.

When Mouse was full, he dozed under the shade of a canopy. Cat crouched in the flower bed, tail up and head down, waiting for his chance.

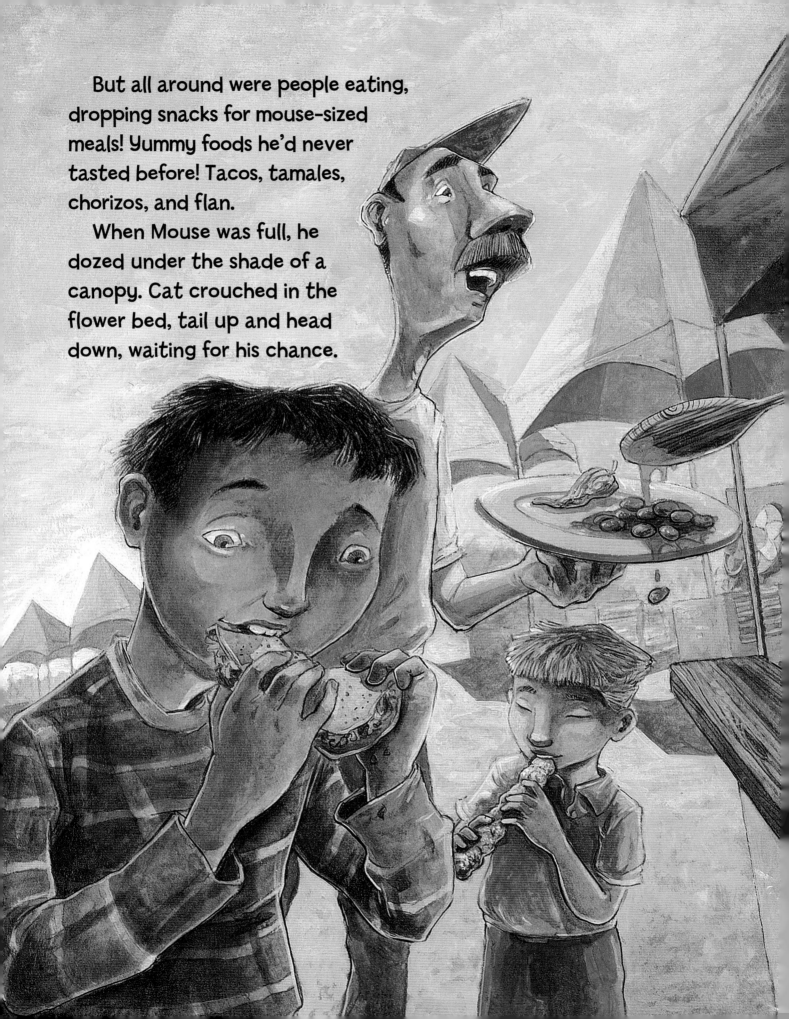

But all around came dancers stamping—heels stomping, toes tapping. Mouse woke up and dashed away from Cat, ducking between dancers' pounding feet, zigging and zagging, jigging and jagging. Cat pounced . . .

. . . but missed his prey as Mouse darted beneath the stage.

Mouse heard the mariachis play—heard the guitarrón, the trumpets, the sweet-voiced violins. Heard the boom of fireworks and people shouting, "¡Viva México!"

When at last Mouse's
heartbeat steadied, his
whiskers quivered. Once again
he smelled the candy hidden
deep in the piñata.

But how to reach the
sweets, buried in the burro,
swaying high above the plaza?

Lickety-split, Mouse scrambled up
the tree. He inched across the rope like a
tightrope walker—one paw in front and
one paw behind.

He didn't see Cat hiding in the daffodils, his
stripy tail switching, his greeny eyes narrowed.

The piñata swayed as Mouse climbed up. He smelled the treats—fruity, sugary, and honey sweet. He nibbled, he gnawed, but he could not reach the treasure inside.

Just then came the swish of the stick as a child swung and someone jerked the piñata aloft.

Mouse held on tight as the piñata swayed and sailed, dipped and spun. A carnival ride for Mouse! In the plaza down below, Cat waited for Mouse to fall into his paws like a ripe plum.

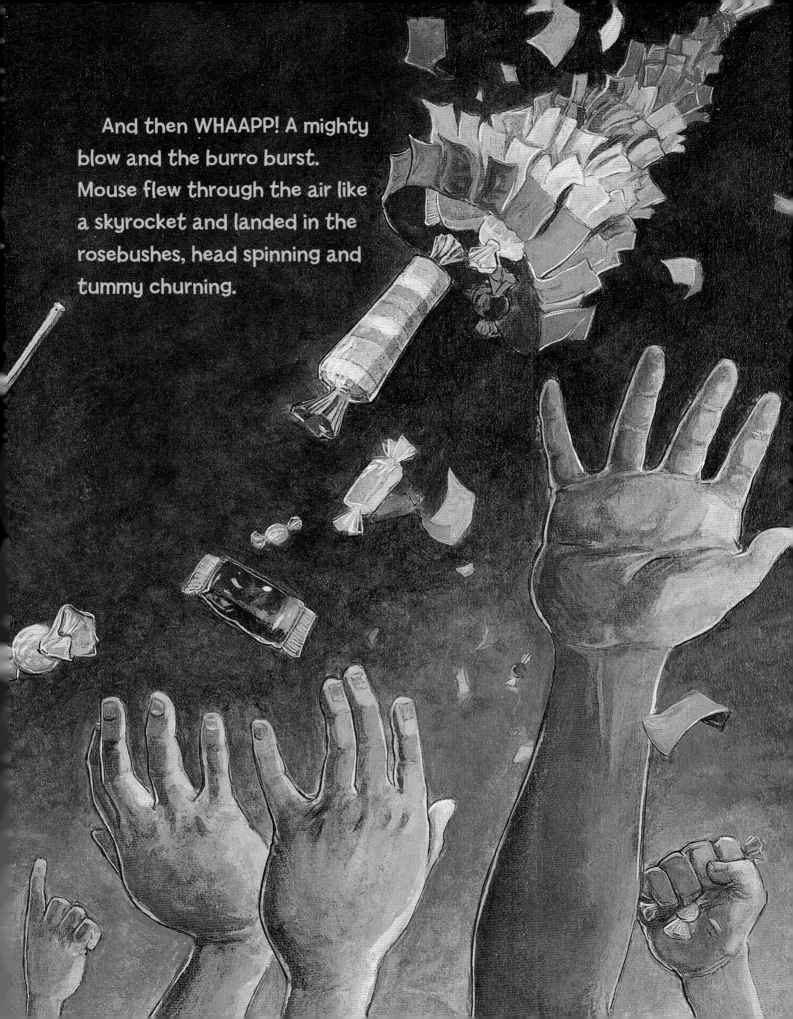

And then WHAAPP! A mighty blow and the burro burst. Mouse flew through the air like a skyrocket and landed in the rosebushes, head spinning and tummy churning.

Candy spilled across the plaza, showering like hailstones. Children ran to and fro, laughing, yelling, and scooping up handfuls, pocketfuls, bagfuls. Someone stepped on Cat's tail and . . .

. . . Cat yowled and sped home, his tail bruised and sore.

When Mouse caught his breath, he sat up. The candy was gone. The people were leaving. The cleaners were sweeping and picking up trash.

No dessert for me, Mouse thought, his whiskers drooping. But wait!

Hidden in the ivy, Mouse spied one lemon drop overlooked, forgotten, and wrapped in shiny cellophane.

He picked it up and ran home to his hidey-hole for one last treat. *¡Cinco de Mouse-O! ¡Qué felicidad!*